To Grace —

Protect our precious oceans!

Merry Christmas 2023 ♡

Blair N. Williamson

FOREWORD

When I was born, plastic in the ocean was not considered to be a problem. Within my lifetime, that has changed. Plastic in the ocean is now one of the major ways humans harm the natural world. Researchers tell us that *over half* of the sea turtle population has accidentally ingested plastic, with one in five not surviving.

Because I care deeply for animals and wanted to do something to protect them, I started the non-profit, Plastic Ocean Project, Inc.

We have three main objectives:

1. To conduct research on plastic to better understand how it impacts nature

2. Create outreach through art to educate the masses about plastic pollution

3. To collaborate with others trying to stop plastic pollution

We lean heavily into the arts, for it is the storytellers who help communicate the science to the public that will help create necessary change.

Most of us can relate to a book we read as a child and how it helped shape our lives. *Island Girls: Free the Sea of Plastic,* based on a situation author Blair Williamson and her family experienced while living on a sailboat, is one such story that will have a lasting positive impact.

Recognizing the importance of what Williamson and her family witnessed, her work—along with the beautiful illustrations—can encourage change by teaching children that they play a key role in removing trash and educating others to do better.

Bonnie Monteleone, Executive Director
Plastic Ocean Project, Inc.

For Sadie and Josie, our beautiful 'island girls'—
Thank you for allowing me to see the joy
of life through your ocean eyes.

H.K.F.H.

Island Girls: Free the Sea of Plastic

Published by
The Island Writer Press

Library of Congress Control Number: 2022945569

ISBN (hardcover): 9781662932472
ISBN (paperback): 9781662932489
eISBN: 9781662932496

Island Girls

Free the Sea of Plastic

BLAIR NORTHEN WILLIAMSON

The Island Writer
Press

Sadie and Josie lived on a sailboat.
They loved all the adventures that came with life at sea.
"Dad! Josie!" Sadie shouted. "We're back from the store!"

After the girls helped put the groceries away,
they skipped to the back of the boat.
Sadie scanned the turquoise water searching
for their turtle friend, Fig.
"There you are!" Sadie said. "What are you munching on?"
SLURRRRRP
"A slimy jellyfish, my favorite!" Fig replied.
"Enjoy your meal!" Josie said.

That night, Sadie and Josie snuggled together.
WHOOSH CLINK CLINK
The wind howled through the anchorage.

The next morning, the girls woke up to a strange noise.
TAP TAP THUD
"Holy anchovies!" Fig cried. "There's trouble in Jellyfish Alley!"
"Josie, get Mom and Dad!" Sadie yelled.

VROOM
The engine roared.

SPLASH

Sadie, Josie, and their mom dove in.
They followed Fig to Jellyfish Alley.

"Look!" Fig said. "The wild wind made a mess."

"These are *our* grocery bags," Sadie groaned.
"They look *just* like jellyfish!"
"They look delicious!" Fig replied.

CLICK CLICK
Josie took pictures.

"Oh no!" Sadie said. "That turtle is stuck!"
He wiggled.
He twisted.
He kicked.
But he couldn't break free.
Until...

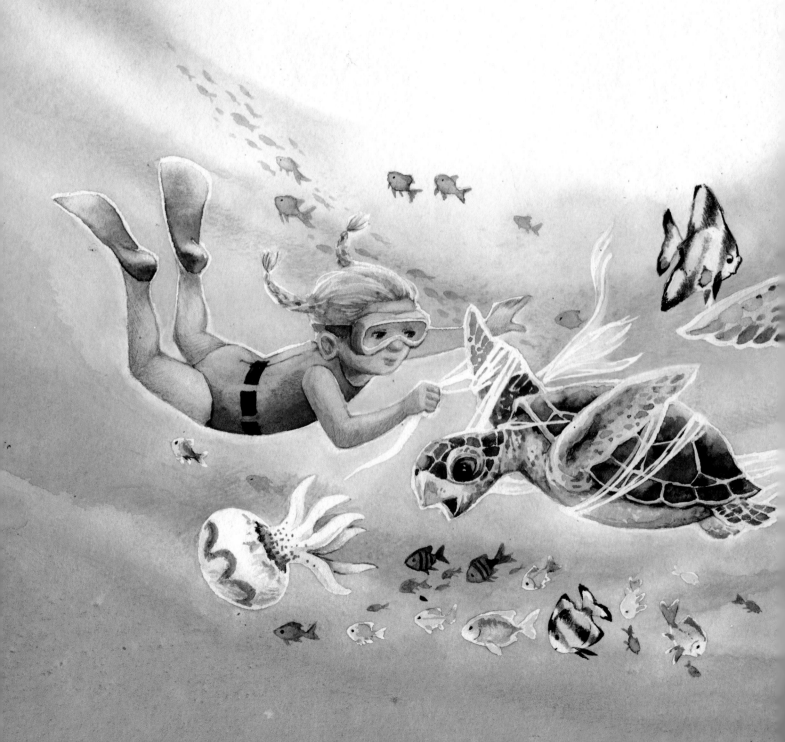

SNIP SNIP

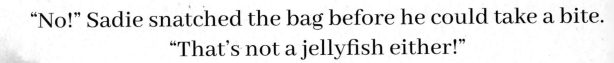

"No!" Sadie snatched the bag before he could take a bite.
"That's not a jellyfish either!"

"Over here, this is your food," Josie said.

"This is bad," Sadie said. "We can't leave this behind."
They got to work.

"It's all clean now. What else can we do?" Sadie asked.
"Oh, I know! We can make signs," Josie suggested. "Jeremy can help."

"Hi, Jeremy! Did you know the turtles are eating plastic bags?" Sadie asked.
"Not again!" Jeremy sighed.
"Can you help us make signs?" Josie asked.
"Of course!" He said.

They cut.
They colored.
They taped.
Until...

BAM BAM BANG
They hung the signs.

FREE THE SEA OF PLASTIC!

"Let's tell everyone," Josie said.

"Great idea, Sis!" Sadie cheered. "I'll write the letters."

"Thanks for your help!" Fig said. "You are turt-ally awesome!"

Well done, island girls.

AUTHOR'S NOTE

This story was inspired by my personal encounters with plastic in the ocean while working as a scuba diving instructor and while snorkeling with my daughters, Sadie, and Josie. We witnessed "Fig" and his young friend, "Zoomy," mistake plastic bags for jellyfish and it left me with an urge to act. I wanted to be a voice for the turtles and speak up on their behalf. Thank you, Svitlana Holovchenko, for bringing this message to life with your beautiful and powerful illustrations. It is my hope that we as humans can work together and free the sea of plastic.
-Blair N. Williamson

A WORD FROM THE ISLAND GIRLS

Dear kids of the world,

Thank you for helping us keep Fig,

Zoomy, and our under-the-sea

friends safe!

Even if you don't live near the ocean,

you can still make a big difference

in their life.

Love,

Sadie and JOSie

*Pictured Sadie and Josie removing plastic bags from the ocean while snorkeling with sea turtles in 2021. Photos copyright B. Williamson

FOR EDUCATORS AND PARENTS
How To Get Kids Involved

1. Have students make their own signs to illustrate how much jellyfish and plastic bags look alike under water
2. Have students write letters to their state senator or representative asking them to ban single-use plastic bags
3. Have students brainstorm other ways they can spread awareness about the dangers of plastics in our oceans

FIND OUT MORE

SUPPORT, VOLUNTEER, DONATE

Plastic Ocean Project. https://www.plasticoceanproject.org/
ActionQuest Summer Programs, British Virgin Islands.
https://www.actionquest.com/adventures/preserving-paradise/
British Virgin Islands National Parks Trust. https://www.bvinpt.org/
Defenders of Wildlife. www.defenders.org/sea-turtles/how-you-can-help

WEBSITES

Visit the National Geographic Kids website to discover more about how kids are fighting plastic. https://kids.nationalgeographic.com/nature/kids-vs-plastic/article/pollution-1

Visit the British Virgin Islands Association of Reef Keepers website for the most up-to-date information on their Sea Turtle Programme http://www.bviark.org/bvi-sea-turtle-programme.html

Follow along author Blair Williamson and the Island Girls' next adventures.
www.theislandwriter.com

About the Author

Blair Northen Williamson is from Richmond, Virginia but spent much of her childhood on the coast of North Carolina where she developed a passion for the ocean. After graduating from the University of Virginia, her love of nature, the ocean, and relating to others led her to work for Global Expeditions Group for over a decade. She spent many years working as a sailing captain and scuba diving instructor in the British Virgin Islands and Southeast Asia, where she experienced the problem of plastics in our oceans too many times. Encouraged by Robert Swan's quote, "The greatest threat to our planet is the belief that someone else will save it," Williamson decided to take action. Seeking to inspire change and empower children by spreading awareness about the danger of plastics in our oceans, Williamson wrote her debut picture book, Island Girls: Free the Sea of Plastic.

About the Illustrator

Svitlana Holovchenko is from Ukraine. Drawing has been her favorite pastime since early childhood. Later, her passion for art became her profession and a tool for self-expression. Nature, traveling and meeting new people is an endless source of inspiration for her. She studied art at design college and worked as a visual designer. One day she had the opportunity to try herself in a new field and it changed her life. She took up illustrating children's books and began working with various publishing houses in Ukraine and Russia. Then her life took another sharp turn. She moved to live in Germany and found herself at the beginning of her new journey. Now she paints pictures, illustrates books and writes her childhood stories, hoping to get them published.